STARLIGHT SAILOR

Barefoot Books
Step inside a story

Star light, star bright,
First star I see tonight,
I wish I may, I wish I might,
Have the wish I wish tonight.

I wish I had a little boat!

Far away I drift and float,

Where the great blue whales leap,

And pirate ships lie sunken deep.

I sail towards another land,
Where children wait on golden sand.

"Over here!" the children say,
"We hope you want to come and play!"

We build a castle
high as high,
With flags that flutter
in the sky,

And let the sea fill up the moat,

Then play upon my little boat.

Up above a bluebird sings,
While we pretend we're knights and kings.

Being very strong and brave,

We go exploring in a cave.

We meet a dragon, red and gold,
Who tells us magic tales of old,

Then stretches both
her wings out wide,

And takes us on
a night-time ride.

We fly across the starlit sky
Until it's time to say goodbye.

Then she brings us down to land
Gently on the golden sand.

Now the children fall asleep.

The dragon curls up at their feet.

I climb aboard my boat once more,

And drift out slowly from the shore.

Starfish swimming in the sea,

Mermaids singing just for me,

I listen to their lullaby,
While flying fish dance in the sky.

Star light, star bright,
First star I see tonight,

I follow you across the night,

through my dreams...

... 'til morning light.

MAKE YOUR OWN PAPER BOAT

Fold a piece of paper in
half towards you.

Fold down the top corners so that
they meet in the middle.

Fold up the bottom edge of
the top sheet of paper.

Next, fold the corners over.

Turn the paper over and do
the same on the other side.

Open out the triangle shape
to make a hat.

Then fold the hat down flat
to form a kite.

Fold the upper bottom point
of the kite up towards the top.

Then turn the paper over
and repeat.

You now have a triangle
shape again

Open the paper out to make a
hat again. Then fold it down the
other way to form a kite again.

Carefully open out the paper
boat by holding the two top
points and pulling them
gently to the sides.

Your boat is now ready
for its first voyage!

Barefoot Books
2067 Massachusetts Ave
Cambridge, MA 02140

Barefoot Books
294 Banbury Road
Oxford, OX2 7ED

Reproduction by B & P International, Hong Kong
Printed in China on 100% acid-free paper
This book was typeset in OneLeigh and Exotica

Text copyright © 2009 by James Mayhew
Illustrations copyright © 2009 by Jackie Morris
The moral rights of James Mayhew and Jackie Morris have been asserted

ISBN 978-1-78285-147-9

British Cataloguing-in-Publication Data: a catalogue record for this book is
available from the British Library
Library of Congress Cataloging-in-Publication Data is available under
LCCN 2008028137
1 3 5 7 9 8 6 4 2